For my friends at Erme Valley, thank you.

'They shall not grow old, as we that are left grow old;
Age shall not weary them, nor the years condemn. *begrimaned*
At the going down of the sun and in the morning,
we will remember them.'

-Laurence Binyon

Dear Emma

Rugglestone Cottage
Stapleton Street
Ashburton
Devon

Miss Emma Clarke
22 Apple Tree Corner
North Tawton
Devon

Dearest Emma,

As I have told you many times before, when I was about your age, I was evacuated from my home in London at the height of World War Two. I was taken to a small village in Devon, not far from where you grew up, and I was placed with a family who lived at Rugglestone Farm, Widecombe-in-the-Moor. I kept a diary of my evacuation; I had been an only child for a while after losing my brother early on in the war, so my diary kept me company, it was almost like a friend. After the war ended and I returned to London, I stopped writing and I never read the diary again. In fact, after that, I packed it away in the attic for many years; I couldn't bear to even see it. But when I was sorting through your Grandmother's things after the funeral, I found it crammed in a cardboard box full of books.

I must admit Emma, I cried buckets the first time I read it through. It brought back so many memories of such a poignant time in my life.

пиканотивый

to cry buckets = to cry a lot

It just made absolute sense that you must read it before anyone else.

I know that you have had your struggles, and in reading my diary,

you will become aware of mine too, but as your Grandmother used

to say, when we are vulnerable together, we are strong, and I know

that she would be so pleased if she knew you had read it. So what

you'll be reading is really my childhood as it happened from March

1941 until I stopped writing in September 1945. I want you to read it

first because I know you will understand. We're the same, you and I,

and I hope that after the heart wrenching few weeks we have had, my

story may bring some light back into your life. I'll be honest, I've

done a fair bit of editing as some parts were too long and boring; I

used to write pages and pages and my grammar was quite poor! But

the surprise comes right at the end, so don't peek Emma. I hope you

enjoy my story, and I hope that it can help you fit together the puzzle

pieces of my life and give back some happiness and understanding to

your own.

Lots of love,

Your affectionate grandfather,

> *Harry*

might he be Rotter?

The Diary of Harry Clarke 1941-1945

Friday March 12th 1941

It's all anyone talks about now, the evacuation. It's like a curse has come down on Hither Green and no one really smiles anymore. We got sent home from school again today. We were sat doing arithmetic with Mrs Parks (which I just can't understand no matter how hard I try) and suddenly there was a huge cracking sound and a big crash and some people outside started screaming. We all ran over to the window and the old corner shop opposite the school was just a huge pile of settling rubble and dust. It was lucky really because Mrs Coombe who owns the shop was out visiting her daughter when it collapsed. I'm really glad she wasn't inside at the time because she's really nice and before rationing she used to give me free strawberry laces. Mrs Parks said that it's happening all over the city now. Bombs from the night before weaken the buildings that are still standing after the raid, and it's only a matter of time before something cracks under the strain and it all comes crashing down. She sent us home just in case but I didn't go home. It was only 1pm and Mum wouldn't be going to work until 4pm so I went for a walk instead. My favourite place in Hither Green to walk is in the park because there are some parts which are far away from the houses and the main road and if no one else is there I can pretend that I'm not in London, and instead it's like I'm far away and no one will ever find me. This is where I came when I ran away from school that time. I sat under the big tree right in the corner of the park and no one found me for hours. It's a safe place. Sometimes I go there to think about Mum and Dad and Jack. I try really hard to think about the time when we went to the fair and dad bought us mint humbugs and then we had fish and chips for tea, or when Dad used to take me and Jack on the bus all around town and we played 'I spy with my little eye' out of the window. It makes me feel better when I remember those things so I just try to think about them all the time. I'm going to think about it now and hopefully it will help me fall asleep and maybe I'll have a dream about Jack and Dad being here and everything would be fine again. I really hope I do.

Monday March 15th 1941

Today at school Mrs Parks had a long list of all the places that we are going when we get evacuated next week. She said we're all going to the West Country which is around a seven hour train journey from London. I couldn't believe it, seven hours! England must be bigger than I thought. My best friends Robert and James are going to a place called Illminster which is in a county called Dorset. Mrs Parks told us that in Dorset there are lots of long beaches full of round pebbles and that maybe Robert and James will learn about boats and fishing. My other friends Charlie and Martha are going to Chagford which is in a place called Dartmoor; and then Mrs Parks said that George and I are going to a place called Ashburton which is also in Dartmoor, so maybe we will get to see each other, and Charlie and Martha too. The other children in my class are going to places in Somerset and Cornwall and a place called Exmoor which is in Devon. Mrs Parks asked us to draw a picture of what we thought our new homes might be like and then we could take them with us and see if we were right. In my picture it was my brother and me sat in a big green field eating mint humbugs and all around us were animals like sheep and cows and chickens and there was a red tractor too, and I thought that me and Jack would drive the tractor back to our home in Dartmoor and then we would have a roast dinner with bread and butter pudding for afters with our new family all around a big table with black and white sheepdogs and horses in stables outside. I was too busy colouring in the tractor that it made me jump when Mrs Parks asked me if I'd like to share my picture. Mrs Parks is kind because I think she knows that sometimes I don't like to show my work to the rest of the class but she helps me. I stood next to her desk and held up my picture facing away from me so the others could see it. I think they liked it, especially the tractor. Charlie said he really hoped that they would have a tractor at his new house and so did Robert. I just smiled because I did too but my voice was shaking too much to say so. Catherine asked who the other boy was in the picture and I looked towards Mrs Parks. She asked me if it was my brother Jack and when I nodded she reached out and squeezed my hand. I brought my picture home with me at the end of school but I haven't show Mum because I don't know if she would want to see it, and anyway she's working now so she was too busy getting ready when I got back. I think I will go to sleep now. I can't believe there's only three nights left before I go to my new home in Dartmoor. I really hope they do have a tractor.

<u>Tuesday March 16th 1941</u>

Last night there was a really bad air raid. I think it was the worst one

yet. It started at about midnight, I could hear some bombs dropping

in the distance but I think I was a bit disorientated at first. I was kind

of half asleep and half awake and for a while I couldn't tell whether I

was awake or in a dream. Sometimes I get like that with the bombs,

it doesn't really feel real, maybe because I can't believe that it is

really happening. Several times I have had dreams with Mum, Dad

and Jack, and we're all in France running away from the frontline

but the mud is thick like treacle and I keep getting stuck. I'm trying

to run, but the more I try, the harder it gets, and then I start to sink. I

start to scream but none of them can hear me and the gunfire and

grenades are getting closer and closer. When I get that dream waking

up in the midst of the blitz is a relief. Anyway, the bombs started

getting closer at around half past midnight and I heard Mum wake

up. She knocked on my door,

"Come on, Harry" she said. "Time to go Harry, bring your blanket, it's freezing outside". I hate getting out of bed in the middle of the night. It's so cold and I hate trudging out across the garden to the shelter, it's so muddy at the moment. We share a shelter with our next door neighbours and they have four children who are all much younger than me. I don't mind really but it's very cramped. When we built it, we didn't think we'd be using it this much, so it's not really very comfortable. I suppose I mustn't complain though, some of the other children in my class don't even have their own shelter so we're very lucky. Sometimes we play card games to try and distract ourselves from the falling bombs all around us, but it's quite dingy and difficult to see, plus when the bombs are really close none of us can concentrate on a card game and we all startle every time we hear a bomb blast. Last night we didn't play any games at all. The bombs fell like rain, everywhere. I wasn't sure if there would be any of London left when we came out, and I was so relieved to see that our little house was still standing at the end of the night. I even managed to get a couple of hours of sleep back in my own bed before getting up for school. It wasn't until I left the house this morning that I realised how bad it was. I knew the bombs were close, but I didn't realise quite how close. Mr and Mrs Wick and their two daughters

Maggie and Jane were sat on the pavement opposite their house; both the girls were crying but luckily nobody had been hurt. Their house was still on fire and I looked up into the sky where ribbons of smoke curled around thick morning mist. They only lived half a street away. I tried to smile at them as I walked past but I wasn't really sure what there was to smile about. The town hall had been bombed too. Luckily nobody was inside but I remembered spending Tuesday evenings there before the war with the cub scouts and I was sad that it was now just a pile of dusty debris. I was so relieved that school hadn't been bombed, and Mrs Parks and the other children in my class were all safe, even the ones who don't have shelters. We did quiet reading all morning; there was a nervous and restless feeling that rippled through the class, I think everybody was a bit frightened really but Mrs Parks knew. She said we'd be safe very soon and at lunchtime she played hide and seek with us outside and it was just the best fun. Mum left me a bowl of stew on the stove for dinner before she left for work, it's one of my favourites even though we can't have dumplings or beef now because of the rationing. I hope we can have dumplings when I get evacuated to Dartmoor because they're so delicious. I'm beginning to feel quite tired but I don't want to go to sleep until I hear Mum come back just in case there's another air raid, I think there probably will be and I want to make sure she is safe. At school James said that the Luftwaffe is going to come every night now until they win the war. I don't know if he's right but I hope he isn't.

I just heard the latch on the door followed by Mum's heels on the floorboards, so I can go to sleep now. I can't believe that tomorrow it will only be two days until I go to Dartmoor.

<u>Thursday March 18th 1941</u>

Mum went to the parents' meeting at the school hall last night. She
doesn't really like to go out when it's dark. I think she gets scared
there might be an air raid, so I waited up for her to get back. She
came back about fifteen minutes ago and she just said all the
children in my class were going (apart from Annie Baker whose
mum has refused) and that we were to meet at Paddington Station at
9am tomorrow morning to catch the first train to the West Country.
She leant against the range and lit a cigarette, and the end glowed
every time she drew a breath.

"You'll be good won't you, Harry? I know you'll be good." She did
her best to smile in my direction but she still looked sad. Mum has
the most amazing sapphire blue eyes but they're mostly glazed over
these days and they don't sparkle like they used to. I smiled back and
came upstairs to pack. I've packed all my things in dad's old suitcase
and it's ready by my bedroom door with my best shoes on top. It all
feels so real now, before it felt a bit like a dream. I will miss my

friends and Mrs Parks too, but she said we won't be away for long. Apparently the war will be over by Christmas, that's what everyone is saying anyway. I really hope there isn't an air raid tonight so I can get some sleep, I've never been on a train before and I want to make sure I stay awake for all of it.

Friday March 19th 1941

Mum was rushing around the house all morning trying to get ready

for work with a cigarette pressed tightly between her lips. She put on

her red lipstick in the reflection of the stove and wore that bright

yellow dress she has with pink flowers and big green leaves on it but

it's a little bit ripped at the bottom now. She put my labels in my

coat pocket and held it up so I could put my arms through the sleeves

and then she kissed me on the forehead, squeezed me tightly, and

left. I know it sounds strange, but I hope she will be happier when

I'm gone. I know she loves me but I think when she looks at me all

she can see is Dad and Jack. I'm just a constant and living reminder

to her of what happened. I see the way she looks at me, and I can't

figure it out. All I know is that her eyes are full of sadness deeper

than the ocean, in a way I've never seen before, and never want to

see again. Mum left at about 8 o'clock so then I walked to school

with my suitcase and waited with some of my friends to get on the

bus to go to Paddington. When I arrived, some of the other mums

were there, and so was Mrs Parks and everyone was very quiet. Lily and Mary were crying and Robert was holding his Mum's hand whilst his little brother clung onto her leg. I didn't really understand. I just tried to block everything else out and kept thinking about my picture and Jack and the tractor and the cows and the sheep and that made me feel better. The train station was very busy. There were lots of other children and their teachers and parents too, so I stayed very close to Mrs Parks so I didn't lose her. We all squeezed our way through the crowds of other children and had to wait quite a while to get our labels checked at the barrier. When we finally got to our platform, Mrs Parks held us all together in her arms and knelt down to speak to us. Around her eyes were red and sore, and her voice cracked,

"I will miss you all every day, but now I can sleep at night knowing you are all safe. Always remember how proud I am of all of you" she said. She cleared her throat, "work hard, and remember everything I have taught you about manners and kindness, and you will be fine". We all hugged and she promised she would see us soon and she couldn't wait to hear about our adventures in the countryside. As we were getting on the train I could see that she had started to cry. Mrs Parks told us once that she doesn't have children.

She said that she couldn't have her own children, but that it was OK because she had us. I think I understand what she means now. We've been on the train for nearly four hours and it's going to start getting dark soon. Robert and James have just got off the train at a place called Yeovil and they're getting on a bus to go to Illminster to meet their new families so I think that means me and George have about one hour left until we get to our place called Ashburton. I have tried so hard to stay awake so that I can see everything out of the window. At first, when we left Paddington, there were just lots of buildings and houses and roads. It was sad because there were so many houses that had been bombed, some were smoking and there was one still on fire. I saw people from my window, sat on the pavement in front of the remains of their homes surrounded by the few belongings they had managed to save and they looked so sad. I know it might sound a little bit selfish but I really hope that doesn't happen to Mum or Mrs Parks. As the train pulled further away from the grey bleakness of London, everything started to change. Grey became green and there were fields and forests bigger than I'd ever seen. It was raining but the sun peeked through milky coloured clouds and made a rainbow that arced over big hills in the distance. I remember thinking maybe we were heading for the pot of gold at the end of the rainbow.

I've been looking out of the window ever since, wondering about

what Rugglestone Farm will be like. I hope Mr and Mrs Starling are

nice, and I hope they have children. It says it's a farm, so I wonder

what animals they have. I've never seen sheep or cows or anything

before except for in books and I'm a little bit nervous, but mostly,

very excited.

On my label it says:

```
Harry Albert Clarke (born: May 4th 1928),
32 Church Road, Hither Green, S. E. London.
Mr and Mrs J.R. Starling,
Rugglestone Farm, Widecombe-in-the-Moor,
Devon.
```

Saturday March 20th 1941

I'm here now at the farm and it's very quiet. I barely got any sleep last night, I was expecting an air raid siren at any time, but of course it never came, and the silence was deafening. My bedsheets stuck to me, I tried to kick them off but I just seemed to get more and more tangled and ended up even more awake, clammy and flustered. I'm worried because I don't think I gave the Starlings a very good first impression and Mrs Parks always said first impressions are important. It was an old man who picked me up from the train station. He said that I can call him Grandpa if I want to, and then he smiled, took my suitcase and we set off away from the platform. It was much smaller than Paddington and there weren't any barriers or people at all. We got on a small cream coloured bus which was very different to the tall red ones in London. There was no clippy standing at the back selling tickets; it was only us and one other lady there. During the journey, the old man quietly told me about Dartmoor and the farm where they live. He said it's a one hundred year old farm just outside a small village called Widecombe-in-the-Moor and there are sheep, cows, pigs, chickens and horses. He said all the animals were his family too, especially his Jersey cows. He said they're his favourite. I met everyone last night when I arrived. By the time we'd walked from the bus stop to the farm it was dark, and the air was bitterly cold. I was glad to get inside the farmhouse. Everyone was stood around the kitchen table looking at me as I cowered by the doorway and two dogs jumped at me barking. I felt that familiar feeling of panic rising in my chest, slowly at first, but before long it seeped into every part of me and clogged up my throat. I squeezed my eyes shut as tight as I could and clamped my hands over my ears to muffle out the barking. I tried to remember what Mrs Parks said to us before we left. A lady led me over to the table, sat me down and made me some tea and toast. She sat next to me and quietly introduced herself, the twins Tommy and Nancy, Grandpa, and the dogs. She said the dogs will get used to me soon, they only barked because they've never seen me before. She asked my name and where I was from, but the words dissolved during the journey from my brain to my mouth and I didn't make any sound at all. I felt my cheeks turn crimson and shrugged before somehow managing to swallow some toast even though it felt like rubbing sandpaper on my throat. I washed it down with tea and the twins showed me to my bedroom.

Sunday March 2^{1st} 1941

Today was a better day. I have made friends with the twins already.
They look exactly the same except Nancy has long curly hair like her
mum and Tommy's is shorter and lighter. I think they are about the
same age as me, maybe a little older, I will ask them one day soon.
Tommy doesn't always say very much, but I think he is kind, and
Nancy is so chatty and bubbly. Tommy helped Grandpa with the
lambing and Nancy spent the morning showing me around the farm
and she never stopped talking the whole time. She showed me all the
animals: the sheep which she called 'Dartmoor Grey Faces', the
cows which were Devon Reds and then the Jersey's which she called
dairy cows. She said they make the best cream in the whole of
Devon. Then she introduced me to the two sheepdogs called Kip and
Oscar and there were pigs and chickens too but I don't think they
had names. My favourite animals though were the horses. They are
kept in stables attached to the side of farmhouse and they are just
perfect. Willow is a beautiful brown mare with a white stripe down

her face and a long blonde mane and tail. Nancy said she used to pull the plough when she was younger. She is really big and strong and I think she looks magnificent. There's also Milly who is a white pony that Nancy rides around the farm and she said that maybe I can ride her one day. I just smiled because I am happy just stroking them and talking to them. I've never seen a horse before, let alone touched one and I don't think there's anything more magical.

Then we went in for lunch all together and Mrs Starling said I can call her Edie. She was busily making sandwiches for everyone and her little spaniel Primrose stayed loyally at her feet the whole time. Primrose is one of the dogs who barked at me last night, but she is beginning to get used to me now and we have made friends. She has long, floppy ears with curly tufts of brown hair at the ends, and dark brown eyes like conkers.

Grandpa seems to be cheerily running the farm whilst his son and Edie's husband is away at war, but I think it's a family effort really; everyone here seems to work really hard. I've barely seen Grandpa or Tommy since I've been here, Nancy says Grandpa is always working out on the farm, from dawn till dusk seven days a week, even Christmas Day.

Tuesday March 23rd 1941

Yesterday was my first day at my new school and I was really

nervous. In Hither Green my school is only just around the corner,

but here at the farm it's a ten minute walk to the bus stop in the

village, then a twenty minute bus ride to Ashburton, then another ten

minute walk through the town to school. I took the same bus ride

with Grandpa when he collected me from the station but it was misty

and beginning to get dark then so I couldn't really see much. This

time it was bright, but drizzly. Nancy said it rains a lot here, she said

Dartmoor is bleak but very beautiful and she glowed with pride

when she said it. I pressed my nose up against the glass window and

peered out across the moorland. Nancy was right, it is beautiful, it's

overwhelmingly beautiful, I'd never seen so much space before. The

biggest space I'd seen was the park at home, but that seemed tiny in

comparison to this. In the distance I could see big hills with rocky

boulders balanced on top of one another, Nancy said they're called

tors and that one is called Haytor. She said they all have their own name and there's 160 of them on Dartmoor. I could hardly believe it, 160! I remember thinking Dartmoor must be a big place. My teacher is called Mrs Edwards and I think she is mostly nice. She wears big round glasses and has blonde hair with loose curls in it. I think she's quite young, much younger than Mrs Parks anyway. Tommy showed me to my classroom this morning and helped me find a peg to hang my things. I was the first person there, so I headed to the back of the room and sat at a desk by the window. Mrs Edwards arrived shortly after and trotted across the front of the classroom juggling bags of books and a container with a sandwich in it. She beamed at me, "Good morning, you must be one of our new arrivals!" Some of the books slipped out of her arms and she caught them clumsily by pressing her knees against her desk.

"What's your name dear?" she said. I opened my mouth as if to speak but the words didn't come and I failed to make any sound at all. Mrs Edwards smiled slightly anxiously, tucked her hair behind her ears and started wiping the blackboard clean for the day. There are four evacuees in my class. There's me, two boys from North London and one girl from Plymouth. There isn't very much space because of us coming so it's a bit crammed in the classroom sometimes. The school is so small, too. It's probably about half the size of my school in London, and there's much less children too, which I like, it's quieter. You can tell who the evacuee children are because they wear their old school uniforms from the city. Edie gave me Tommy's old school jumper to wear though which was kind because I really don't want to stand out; I don't have a tie but Edie said Mrs Edwards wouldn't mind.

Tommy and Nancy aren't in my class; they're one year older than me so I don't see them apart from at break-time and lunch-time. Nancy came to find me yesterday and today and she said I could stay with her. She's kind and friendly and very popular and all her friends call her 'Nan' for short. I think maybe I will stick with her at school. I don't think the other children in my class like me very much they kept calling me a townie today and I really don't like it.

<u>Friday March 26th 1941</u>

I've been here for nearly a week now and I think I'm beginning to settle in. It's so quiet, it's strange. I keep expecting to hear an air raid siren, or bomb blasts, but of course, they never come. It was eerie to begin with and I struggled to get used to it, but I think it's fine now. I've tried not to think too much about London and home. Mum will be keeping herself busy working and Mrs Parks said she was going to paint and redecorate the whole classroom whilst we were away. I can't wait to see what it looks like when we get back. I've spent quite a lot of time up here in my bedroom. The floorboards are so old and creaky, they groan even when I tip-toe and I don't want anyone to hear me. The twins help out on the farm after school until supper time, but I don't want to get in anyone's way, so I usually come upstairs and practise my arithmetic or writing on the bed until Edie calls out for supper. It was about 5 o'clock because I could hear the cows walking across the yard outside my window to be milked for the evening. I slipped out from under the duvet, crept across the room and peered out of the window. It had finally stopped raining.

The whole sky was a chalky pink colour and amber clouds reflected in the puddles on the ground. I could hear Tommy and Grandpa chatting to the cows and the distant hum of the radio in the parlour. That's when I heard a faint knocking on my bedroom door. It was Nancy. She bounced into my room and asked me if I wanted to help her bottle feed a couple of the orphaned lambs. I don't think I could contain the grin that spread across my face and I slipped on my boots and followed her out onto the farm.

<u>Monday March 29th 1941</u>

I know I've only been here for a short while but it feels like I've been here forever. I've now learnt how to bottle feed the lambs and how to look after the horses. The horses eat hay, which is like dried grass, and they also get a bucket of oats each morning; they smell like syrup and the horses love them. After I've given them their oats I muck out the stables and give them fresh straw for the day, and if the weather is good then they can go in the paddock behind the house until after school. Then, when I come home from school, I grab their halters and run straight to the paddock to fetch them. Milly always spots me first and she comes trotting over to the gateway nickering at me and shaking her head excitedly. Then Willow comes, more calmly than cheeky Milly. She plods towards me and whinnies gently. I didn't know animals could smile, but I'm almost sure Willow does. Nancy often goes out riding on Milly after school, she said today that I could go too but I'm still a little nervous about riding so I said I'd stay and help feed the lambs instead. I've never ridden a horse before and Willow is really quite big. It's Friday

today and Edie told me that she always cooks a special tea on

Fridays. Edie and grandpa grow a lot of their own vegetables, and of

course eggs, milk and cream are in abundance because of the

chickens and Jersey cows, so we have much more to eat than I have

done since before the war started. Edie say's they're very lucky and

it's true, in London the rationing was so strict, before I came to

Devon I can't remember the last time we had cream, and this week

I've had it twice on home-grown stewed apples for pudding. It was

delicious. Tonight though, Edie cooked Tommy's favourite, egg and

sausage pie with rhubarb crumble for pudding. It was really great, I

tried not to eat it too quickly but I couldn't help myself and I even

had second helpings of the crumble. When I was in London I always

tried to give the best food to Mum so I think now I am really very

hungry. Afterwards, Nancy lit the fire and we sat in the living room

and played monopoly and it was just so much fun. Grandpa won and

Nancy was stroppy because she kept rolling unlucky numbers on the

dice. It was quite funny really because Tommy was making fun of

her, saying she's too competitive and that it's only a game, Edie just

smiled as Grandpa took yet more paper money from Nancy until she had none left at all. I am in bed now with a very full tummy and lots of cosy blankets and I am counting myself very lucky indeed. Edie said that I can pick my favourite tea for everybody to eat next Friday and I'm not sure what I will choose. Maybe stew (with dumplings!) or maybe Woolton pie, I really love toad-in-the-hole too, but I don't know if we'll be able to have sausages again because we had them today. I will definitely choose bread and butter pudding for dessert though, that was mine and Jack's favourite, especially with crunchy brown sugar sprinkled on top. Delicious.

<u>Wednesday March 31st 1941</u>

My second week in Devon is going well so far. I didn't even know
that Dartmoor or anything here existed before and I can't tell you
how much I was missing out. It's truly wonderful, there's nothing
quite like it. The evenings are beginning to draw out a little longer
each day, and after tea, I like to go for a walk. Sometimes Tommy or
Nancy come, and sometimes Primrose and the sheepdogs come, but
today I went on my own. I walked to the village and sat on a wooden
bench on the green. I just sat for a while listening to the birds
singing. They sounded like their very own orchestra, high pitched
chirps blended with the deep rhythmical knocking of a woodpecker,
the gentle tweets of tiny garden birds and the distant screeching of a
tawny owl or maybe a barn owl. I didn't know anything at all about
birds before I came here because I never really heard them in
London. There were far too many other noises, but Grandpa loves
birds and he taught me all about them. We stood out in the farmyard
a few mornings ago and he taught me all the different songs, well the

ones we heard anyway. I learnt the song of blackbirds, robins, owls and woodpeckers. Since then I've been practising and I've learnt a few new ones too.

I learnt how to drive the tractor today! I just can't stop smiling. I've

smiled so much my cheeks ache but it's totally worth it. The sun

shone all day yesterday and today so Grandpa decided it was a good

day to get out in the fields and spread some muck on the ground

whilst it was dry. Grandpa said that the cow muck is perfect for

fertilising the fields and helping the maize grow ready for harvest in

September. I have to admit the smell was so strong I found it hard to

breathe at first, and I was trying to cover my nose with my shirt.

Tommy noticed and smiled to himself,

"You won't smell it before long, Harry, you'll get used to it" he said.

I'm not sure I believe him; I can still smell it now and I've had a

bath and everything. Anyway, I was just helping Tommy check the

calves this morning when Grandpa came in and asked to borrow me

for a moment. I followed him out onto the yard and he opened up the

little shed where the tractor is kept overnight. Grandpa loves his

tractor. Nancy told me that he calls her Bessie and he always washes her down at the end of each day and polishes her on a Sunday. He says it's important so she doesn't get rusty. He said he had to sell a lot of pigs to be able to afford her and he was going to make sure he looked after her. Bessie is bright red like a London bus with tyres bigger than I've ever seen. She has a blue grill on the front and a black seat towards the back which is set on springs. I guess driving a tractor in the fields can be pretty bumpy sometimes. Grandpa sat up on the seat and started her up. She coughed and spluttered for a little while but then came alive and started chugging away. It was louder than I thought and I had to fight the urge to cover my ears. Grandpa beckoned me over and patted his lap.

"Come on then Harry, your turn" he said, and before I had a chance to think about it I leapt up and squeezed on the little seat next to him. I don't remember ever being so excited in my whole life and I remember waving and grinning enthusiastically at Edie and Nancy through the kitchen window as we headed out of the yard towards the fields above the church. Grandpa and I were out on the field all afternoon and he never stopped talking the whole time. He told me all about the farm and how it was when he was a boy. He's lived on Rugglestone farm his whole life you know, and he said when he was little nobody had tractors, just horses, like Willow. He told me about

his family, he'd married a neighbouring farmer's daughter, Jane, and

together they had three sons. There was the eldest James, who is

Tommy and Nancy's dad, then Robert, and the youngest was

William. He said Robert lives in Plymouth with his family and

works on the dockyard fixing ships, and that William is a teacher at a

boarding school in North Devon. He beamed when he spoke about

them and he sounded very proud. He went a little quiet after that and

told me that his wife Jane had died when the boys were quite young,

she had a heart problem and had died in her sleep. I told him that my

dad had died too and my brother, he smiled at me and we carried on

bumping across the field watching the sun melt into the horizon. By

the time we got back it was dark and there were more stars in the sky

than I'd ever seen before. I gazed up at them as Grandpa put Bessie

away and I thought about Mum. I wondered if she was in Hither

Green looking up at the same stars. Before the war you couldn't see

many stars in London because the sky was always so thick with

pollution but it had got better since the blackout and Mum loved to

stargaze. The longer I looked, the more seemed to appear, billions,

(maybe even trillions) of tiny specks of sparkling dust surrounding our little planet. It made me feel safe knowing that I am only a moment, not even the blink of an eye, the tiniest dot of something in a never ending universe. I suppose that might scare some people but I find it comforting, to know that what I've done and what I'm doing probably means nothing at all.

<u>Monday April 5th 1941</u>

Today wasn't a good day. I knew it wouldn't be because yesterday was a year since Dad got killed in France and I really miss him. I kept thinking about Mum in Hither Green on her own and I felt weighed down with guilt. I wondered if she ever thought about me but I know deep inside that she probably doesn't. I think today also started off badly because I didn't really sleep very well. Grandpa, Tommy and Nancy were out on the farm most of the night because they're really busy with lambing at the moment. I don't know how to help with the lambing and I was scared I might just be in everyone's way, so I stayed inside. I lay in bed awake listening to the hubbub in the barn, and every time I heard a new-born lamb begin to bleat for its mother I felt all tingly inside. By the time morning came, Tommy and Nancy were both exhausted and I felt guilty for not helping. Even Nancy was quiet on the bus to school and I wanted to ask her if she was OK but I was too scared so I didn't. We went our separate ways at the school gate and I managed to keep my head down until I got to class. All I had to do was get through the day and then I could go back to Rugglestone and sit with Willow and Milly or perhaps take Primrose out for a walk, and they would make everything better again. The first lesson of the day was Biology which is my favourite so that made me feel a bit better but then the bad bit came after that. It was English and Mrs Edwards wanted us to write a story about our homes and where we're from. She said it would be really interesting because some people in the class come from different places now because of the war and being evacuated. So I tried my best even though writing is hard, and I wrote what I could about Hither Green and my house on Church Road. I wrote about the red brick houses all in long rows with slate roofs, the covered up street signs and home-made blackout blinds. I wrote about the air raid shelters in everyone's gardens, the sirens echoing through the streets and the bombed out buildings everywhere you looked. I wrote about my old school and Mrs Parks and suddenly I missed her so much my tummy ached. I tried to remember everything I could from London and Hither Green but even though I hadn't been there long ago, it all just seemed a smoggy blur of sadness and it was hard to go back there even though it was just my imagination. I realised then just how much my life had changed in the short time I'd been in Devon with the Starling's. I couldn't imagine ever going back to London and the thought of it filled me with a fear I'd never felt before. All I needed was for Mum and Mrs Parks to be here too in Ashburton and everything would be perfect and we'd never have to go back to London ever again. I started to doodle to try and drown myself in a happier daydream. I drew a little river, swirling around the page and flowing out into the ocean over the margins of the page. It ebbed and flowed between the lines and I drew a small boat bobbing up and down on its very own ink sea. I started to feel calmer and I drew some little fish darting around the river too. Mrs Edwards hauled me back to reality when she said it was my turn next to share my piece. I didn't quite hear her at first, but when it clocked, I felt a sudden and deep dread that spread all over my body and made me feel sick. I wished Mrs Parks was there, but she wasn't. It was just me, and a classroom full of children who considered me a strange townie. I made my way to the front of the class and stood in front of the blackboard. I took a deep breath as if to start, but I couldn't make a sound and I felt my cheeks begin to burn, I pulled my sleeves over my hands as though to try and hide from them all. I swallowed and tried once more. I felt a lump rising in my throat and before I could do anything to stop them, tears started streaming down my face. A quiet snigger rippled through the room and everyone was staring at me. There I was, stood there in my oversized, borrowed school jumper unable to read out my work. Shame and embarrassment flooded my lungs and before I could even think, I grabbed my bag and ran for the door. Without stopping I ran and ran. I ran until I couldn't see the school anymore, I ran through the streets of the town and everyone was looking at me but I didn't care I just kept running. I ran through the woods onto the moor. I didn't know where I was but I had to get away and I kept running and running until I could barely breathe. Dartmoor is so big, you can see so far in to the distance across empty stretches of amber moorland; I felt so small and frightened. I stumbled through thick bracken and heather and squelched through peaty bogs until I reached a cluster of boulders. It felt like I had been running for hours and I was exhausted. I glanced around; I couldn't see anybody, only several grey sheep tearing at the thick grass nearby. I just crouched and huddled behind a rock. I tried to take control of my breathing. I clamped my hands over my ears and listen to the muffled regularity of my heartbeat. That always calms me down. I don't remember how long I was there before I heard the distant juddering of an engine. I peered over the rock and a Land Rover was chugging along the lane not far from where I was hiding. It was coming towards me. I was so scared the driver might see me and take me back to school. I looked around and saw a tor in the distance, it wasn't Haytor, it was smaller and I could see some trees around it and I thought that maybe I could hide beneath them. I waited for the right moment and ran. I was running alongside a mossy drystone wall and I looked back over my shoulder to see where the Land Rover was. I hoped that perhaps the driver hadn't seen me and that was the last thing I remember. I felt my foot get caught in the undergrowth and I fell. A sharp pain ripped through my skull. Then everything went black. Time passed by but I don't know how much. I don't really remember what happened next but Nancy and Tommy were there when I woke up and Nancy had wrapped my head with Tommy's sweater. A thick fog was rolling in across the moor and I could smell the muskiness of damp bracken and gorse. It was getting dark, the visibility was getting worse and worse and I was so cold I was shivering violently. Tommy and Nancy helped me to my feet, blood saturated Tommy's sweater and dripped down my face. I felt so sick. Nancy told Tommy to run back along the road to find Grandpa and Edie. She sounded worried. She said everyone in the village had been looking for me ever since Mrs Edwards had rung Edie and told her I'd run away. I felt so guilty, all this over telling a story to the class. I swore to myself I would never run again over something so silly. My head throbbed and I was sick. The next thing I remember, I was back at the farmhouse sat at the kitchen table, my head being stitched up by a doctor. I was scared that Edie and everyone would be really cross because Mum always used to get so angry when I ran away from school at Hither Green, but they weren't. Edie hugged me so tightly and said she was so glad that the twins had found me and that I was safe. Then when the doctor left, she sat by the stove and made hot chocolate and gave me a blanket. Then she wiped the blood off my face and gently brushed it out of my hair. Tommy and Nancy came in and Nancy gave me a hug and Tommy smiled sheepishly and said he would teach me how to milk the cows if I wanted. I smiled and nodded and then out of nowhere, the tears started streaming down my cheeks again. But these were a different sort of tears. For the first time no one was cross with me, they seemed to understand, and for the first time in such a long time,

I felt safe. That was yesterday and I've spent most of today in bed. Edie brought Primrose up to my room and I've been cuddling her and stroking her velvety coat. Edie said dogs always make us feel better and I think it's true. My head still hurts today, but I feel less sick, and I managed to eat some bread and soup at lunch time. Tommy and Nancy came to see me after school. They sat on the end of my bed and Nancy chatted and chatted about her day and how exciting last night was. She said it was the talk of the school, that the evacuee boy ran all the way from Ashburton to the moor. I sunk into the bed with embarrassment, I felt so silly that everybody had been out looking for me and I couldn't stop apologising. Nancy laughed and hugged me tight, she said it didn't matter and Tommy said everyone was just so relieved that I was safe.

I think I will have to finish writing this tomorrow because it's now nearly midnight and after everything that's happened I just need to sleep. I am quite scared about going back to school but Edie said I need a couple of days off because I've had quite a bad concussion. She said she will take Tommy and Nancy to school tomorrow and speak to Mrs Edwards first thing in the morning and explain everything to her. I love Edie already; she's so nice to me.

Thursday April 8th 1941

I haven't gone back to school yet but I don't really mind. I have been

spending the days helping Edie and Grandpa around the farm, and

Edie has been teaching me to cook too. Last night I made tea for

everybody all by myself for the first time ever and it was so much

fun. I think everyone enjoyed it too. I boiled little new potatoes with

butter and salt and roasted some carrots in the aga and then Edie

helped me cut some chunks of fish and mix them in a sauce that we

made with cream and some dried herbs. We eat a lot of fish here

because it isn't rationed and because we're so close to the sea Edie

gets it very fresh from Ashburton market. I think it's quite tasty but

Nancy doesn't really like it, I think she liked it in the cream sauce

though. Then for pudding I made almond biscuits, Edie had to help

me a lot because I've never baked anything before but I think

everyone enjoyed them. Grandpa said they were delicious and

Tommy had two. It's been raining all week which always makes

work harder out on the farm because the animals hate being wet and cold and there's so much mud everywhere. I've never seen so much mud in my life before I came to Devon. Because of the rain the sheep and the cows have been spending a lot more time in the barns which means lots more mucking out and feeding so it's been very busy. Edie says I mustn't do too much because of my head but I actually feel fine and I've really loved helping them whilst Tommy and Nancy are at school. Sometimes, because I don't know much about farming yet, I feel like I'm not very useful and that maybe I just get in the way a little bit, but this week I think I've learnt a lot and now I can do lots of jobs on my own and that makes me really happy.

It's been nearly a week since I hit my head and I'm really starting to feel much better. I had my stitches taken out yesterday evening and I have a pretty big scar on my right temple but it doesn't hurt or anything. When Nancy saw it first she laughed and said all the girls at school will fancy me when I go back. I wasn't really sure if she was joking or not so I just smiled. I've been sitting with Willow and Milly in the stables this evening because I was a little bit nervous about the doctor coming again. I love chatting to Willow and just sitting and listening to them both munching on their hay. When I was in the stable this evening Willow started pawing the ground at her straw and then she lay down next to me. At first I was a little bit taken aback but after a few minutes I shuffled closer to her and cuddled into her. She was so warm and soft and her coat smelled musky and like sweet haylage, it was perfect. I rested my head against her side and beneath me I could feel her ribcage softly rising and falling as she breathed. I'm not sure how long I was there but after a while I heard the doctor's car pull up on the yard, so I took a deep breath, kissed Willow goodnight, and went inside. Edie said I can probably go back to school on Monday and believe it or not, I'm not actually that afraid of going.

<u>Monday April 12th 1941</u>

Today was my first day back at school after hitting my head. Edie came with me and she spoke to Mrs Williams who is the head teacher. I don't know what she said because they spoke just the two of them, but when I went back to class everyone was much kinder than I thought they would be and no one asked me why I ran away. We did science and maths and when Mrs Edwards asked the class a question I even put my hand up to answer. At lunch-time Nancy and Tommy came and found me and we ate together, just the three of us, we chatted on the field, and Nancy made daisy chain necklaces. It seems strange to me when I remember that I've only been here in Devon for a month. To me it seems like I've been here, and known Tommy and Nancy forever. London feels worlds away and sometimes it makes me feel guilty that I don't miss it at all, in fact, I dread going back. I'm trying really hard not to think about everything that happened with Dad and Jack because it was really hard but it keeps slipping back into my mind and it won't go. I haven't really thought much about it since I came to Devon, but

since my accident I can't stop thinking about them. I was so lucky

that there were kind people looking for me when I was hurt, and

there to help me get better. But what if Dad and Jack didn't have

anyone to help them? I am trying not to think about it, but I am

scared that maybe they died alone.

Tommy and Nancy got letters from their dad today. We'd just
arrived home from school, Nancy was teasing Tommy and he
jokingly flicked some mud at her and she squealed and bounced
around the yard giggling. Tommy just winked and smiled at me as
we headed into the house and I grinned back. Edie was clutching a
buddle of letters in one hand and holding on to the stove rail with the
other. Her eyes were glazed over and her cheeks slightly red as
though she had been crying. For just a moment there was a
frightening silence and I felt a surge of panic begin to crawl up my
spine. Then she smiled and held up the letters for Tommy to see.
"It's OK Tommy", she said. "Your Dad is fine, he's sent letters for
us all". I tried to hide the relief that poured out of my lungs. I
swallowed back the panic. It was fine and James was fine. We all sat
around the table and I listened as each of them read their letters
aloud. Edie busied herself cooking tea whilst she listened, and as the
twins read their letters she smiled endearingly and glowed with
happiness. Tommy and Nancy's dad is called James (I think I've

mentioned him before) and he's an engineer in the Army too just like my brother was. He said in his letter to Tommy that the tanks break down a lot and it's so muddy that they always get stuck too. He said the Jerry's are persistent and they're bombed everything they can in France, and that the French have lost everything. He said there's hardly any of it left, no towns, barely any villages, it's all just a mass of rubble and ruins, but us English are strong, he said, and we won't give in. He said that he was really missing Edie's home cooking and he couldn't wait for a Devon roast dinner. He wrote to Nancy that all of their food is concentrated, even tea, milk and sugar come in blocks, you just have to add hot water, and he said he has never eaten so many biscuits in his life since he came to France, he said they're not very nice but 'beggars can't be choosers', which made me smile. He said that they have a wireless and they spend a lot of their time sitting in muddy trenches listening to music. He wrote "The music reminds me of happier times Nancy, back on the farm with all of you and I long to be home, but I know I will be soon". I felt an empty, hollow kind of feeling when I was listening to the twins reading their letters. I was so glad that James was alive and well and it made me feel all tingly inside to see the twins, Edie and

Grandpa so happy. But I couldn't help feel a bit of jealousy, and I loathed myself for it. I came up to bed early this evening, it was hard being happy for the Starling's when my reality is so different. What I would give for a letter from my Dad, or my brother. I think Edie knew because she just brought me a mug of hot milk and toast with jam. She came in and sat on the end of my bed,

"You're a very brave young lad, Harry, you know that don't you?" she said, and she stroked my cheek, said goodnight and left.

Today was just so much fun. We did all the animals this morning

and went off to school as usual, and everything was fine. It was a

good day, we did maths and science and after lunch we learnt about

other countries all over the world and it was just amazing. Anyway

what happened was, we were on the bus home, just chugging up the

hill out of Ashburton and onto the moor, when the bus made a big

clunking noise and just stopped! Mrs Ellice the bus driver tried and

tried to start it up again but it just wouldn't, something was broken

and we were stuck. Mrs Ellice said we would have to walk either

back to Ashburton or make our own way home, so Tommy said it

wasn't that far, and that we should walk home. So we did. It was the

warmest and clearest day of spring so far I would say, and when we

walked up over the moor, you could see for miles and miles. There

were pearly snowdrops sprouting out of the ground, and the gorse

was golden and smelt of honey; it was just perfect. Normally in

Hither Green, there are too many houses in the way to be able to see very far and the chimneys are always puffing thick smoke into the sky, so this was just amazing. Nancy laughed at me and said that my face was a picture. I'd never heard that saying before so I didn't really know what she meant but I smiled anyway and she smiled back and bounced across a little stream like a deer. Our school shoes weren't very good for walking across the moor and we got a bit wet from the boggy bits but it didn't matter. Tommy told me all the places we walked past, Holwell Lawns, Haytor, Hound Tor rocks, then we crossed the East Webburn River and Bonehill Rocks and some other places too but I can't remember their names now. We chatted and laughed the whole way and I've never felt happier.

It was about 5 o'clock by the time we got back to the farm and suddenly I felt very tired. We went out onto the yard and helped Grandpa with the evening milk whilst Nancy and Edie fed the calves and then we all sat around the kitchen table and exchanged stories from our day. Edie made us hot milk and toast with homemade jam for supper and we sat by the stove and chatted and chatted about our adventures on the moor and suddenly I didn't feel tired anymore. I just wanted to be there with them in that moment forever and ever, I never want any of this to end.

<u>Monday April 19th 1941</u>

Nancy, Tommy and I all walked to church together yesterday, just us

three for the first time since I've been here. Nancy chatted away like

she does about this that and the other, and Tommy and I just listened

and smiled (like we do). It was one of those mornings where white

mist hung in the valley and cloaked the fields and moorland all

around us and all we could hear was the bleating of lambs and it was

so peaceful. There were no air raid sirens, no noisy red buses or

rhythmically clunking trains, no bombs in the night and no noisy

people everywhere. It was just us and Dartmoor and I guess it was

then whilst I was looking around at everything and just being there

with the twins that I realised this was home. But I've been thinking

and I think home is more than a place. The Starling family are home,

too, Tommy and Nancy, Edie, and Grandpa, Primrose, Willow and

Milly, and all the animals on the farm. I know I've only been here

for a short while, but I really think this is where I belong. I'm not

scared anymore, I've got Edie, she cares for me and looks after me, and I've got Tommy and Nancy. They helped me when I was frightened and lost in the middle of the moor and they didn't shout at me or get cross with me for running away. Instead they hugged me until I stopped crying and took me home and said it would all be OK. I guess what I'm trying to say is you don't really realise how much you need something until it is right in front of you, and then you see that actually you've been missing it all along. I'm not sure if that makes sense really but I suppose this is my diary so it doesn't really matter because I know what I mean.

These are all the things that were flying around my head whilst we were all sat in church this morning so I feel a bit naughty now for not concentrating on what Reverend Johns was saying but I suppose it was important for me to realise these things too and churches are good places for lots of thinking. Anyway, it's getting dark here and I've just heard Grandpa come in from the evening milk so I'd better try and get some sleep. I'm not frightened to go to school tomorrow anymore, I'm not frightened of anything.

I'm sorry I haven't written for a couple of days, I've been so busy on

the farm with Grandpa, Tommy and Nancy. Lots of calves are being

born at the moment and they are so adorable. A pair of Jersey cow

twins were born last night, and Grandpa said I can choose their

names. They're both a dark caramel colour with fluffy blonde ears

and tiny black hooves and they are just perfect. I've decided to call

them Bella and Honey and this evening I helped Tommy to bottle

feed them. I love the sound of them sucking and slurping at the milk,

and when they've finished, they always have frothy milk around

their lips and it's just the sweetest thing. I've also been riding

Willow almost every day because Nancy and I have been using the

horses to round the sheep up in the evenings. Milly is much more

agile than Willow, and she darts and dashes around the field at the

speed of light whilst Nancy rides her so effortlessly, it's as though

they are one. I think Willow prefers to calmly watch on, she doesn't

care much for racing around like Milly does. If Willow was a human

I know we'd be the best of friends.

Today is a day I don't think I will ever forget for as long as I live.
The morning started normally, Tommy and I helped grandpa feed
the animals before school and then I helped Edie muck out Willow
and Milly's stables and walk them out to the paddock. I could tell it
was going to be a hot day because the morning air hung heavy over
the moorland, and on the horizon the fields were blurred with haze.
The school day passed by, and it wasn't long before the three of us
were back on the bus chugging up the hill out of Ashburton towards
home. Nancy was sat on the bench in front of Tommy and I, and she
turned around and grinned at me sheepishly.

"Fancy a ride this evening Harry?" she said. We'd been riding a lot
recently, mostly to help with the sheep, but sometimes when we had
enough time we'd escape up onto the moor and it was just magical. I
loved riding Willow best, and Nancy rode Milly. We rushed home to
try get all our jobs done on the farm so we could ride out before
dark, and just as we started feeding the lambs, Grandpa came in and
said he'd finish up for us. I beamed at Nancy and she squealed with

excitement before we both ran into the farmhouse to get changed.

Negotiating the winding track up out of the village is always the hardest part. Peaty water rushes off the moor over large slabs of granite either side of the path and the cushions of moss that creep over everything make it slippery going. The horses' hooves clattered rhythmically on the stone and they breathed heavily as we clambered up onto the moor. Nancy chatted the whole time, I wasn't sure whether she was talking to me or Milly, but I'm not sure she really knew either and she continued chatting away. When we reached the top of the hill, the track ended and opened up onto moorland. I peered between Willow's pricked brown ears and looked down across the hill towards Ashburton. The farmland beyond the town was quilted together by hedgerows, tracks and lanes connecting the villages like a dot to dot all the way to the sea on the horizon. We turned towards Haytor and trotted until we met the road. Milly pranced and bounced around and Nancy giggled,

"I think she wants to gallop, Harry", Milly snorted and Nancy grinned. I'd only galloped on Willow once before, the previous week, but I had really loved it. There's nothing quite like it, I've never been so fast in my life before. I think it's even faster than when I was on the train. It feels like it anyway. The air whooshes past your ears and Willows hooves thunder on the ground. I can feel her heartbeat beneath me as she breathes heavily; it makes me feel on top of the world. Nancy turned parallel to the road and Milly leapt forward excitedly. Nancy clicked at her and she sprung into a bouncy canter. Willow is much calmer than Milly, but even she was keen to go and it wasn't long before I was cantering alongside Milly and Nancy. The horses bounded across the moor for what felt like an eternity, and it wasn't until we met the river that we pulled them up for a paddle and a drink. We dismounted, giddy from the excitement, and sat on the river bank whilst the horses cooled off in the water. The light was beginning to fade into a dusky lilac and the temperature had dropped, it was getting cold. We just chatted and laughed as the sun went down and I remember thinking I wanted to stay in that moment forever. It was then that I heard it. Distant at first, but it rumbled closer and closer, a terrifyingly familiar sound that I hoped I'd never hear again. The horses stopped drinking and pricked their ears, they were suddenly alert and tense, Milly snorted anxiously. Nancy looked at me, puzzled by the sound,

"What is that Harry?" I knew exactly what it was, and I felt terror that I hadn't felt for months. I covered my ears, curled up into a ball and started to scream. I'd never seen Nancy frightened before, but as the roar of the engines became unbearably loud, the horses panicked and fled back towards the farm and Nancy glanced at me, her face was suddenly pale and deep with fear. She yelped and tried to run after them but then it happened and she fell to the floor. I don't really remember the minutes that followed. I never saw the plane crash but I heard it that's for sure, and the crackle of flames and pillows of smoke led us to where it had hit the ground. It was just a ball of flames; I couldn't see the cockpit at all. Nancy clung to me crying, "Harry we have to go get help". Her voice squeaked with terror. I couldn't just leave it, what if someone was in there and needed our help? I thought of Dad and Jack, and I knew what I had to do.

"Run back to the village Nancy, run as fast as you can, someone must have heard it crash, tell them we need help". I kissed her on the forehead and she whimpered, her eyes swollen with tears. "Go, Nancy", and without another thought she turned and ran. The flames crackled and spat and I took a deep breath before moving closer towards the wreckage. It wasn't until I got closer that I saw the black crosses on the wings and suddenly I felt sick to the core. I swallowed

back the panic and clambered up onto the left wing, I crawled along

the top of it, trying to get a peek inside the cockpit. The smoke stung

my eyes and I jumped out of my skin every time a spark popped but

I couldn't see anyone. The cockpit glass was smashed and the

controls were burning. The seat was burnt but empty and there

wasn't anybody in the foot well either. I leapt off the wing and

sprinted back across the moor as quickly as I could and I never

looked back once. I was running up the hill the other side of the river

and I stopped for a moment to catch my breath. That's when I saw

him. He was cowering beneath a tree, trembling. His parachute was

still attached to his jacket, but it was tangled in the branches above

him and he was stuck. I froze. I glanced around, Nancy had been

gone for what felt like hours, where was she? I thought she was

getting help? The ground was spongy and peaty and I could smell

the burning oil from the wreckage. It leached into my lungs like

treacle and hung heavy in the air. He hadn't seen me yet. He tore his

leather hat and gas mask off and pressed the back of his head against

the tree trunk gasping like a fish out of water. His hair was yellow

blonde, but oily, and his face thin and pale. He didn't look much older than me. I didn't speak, I just moved slowly towards him trying to ignore the anxiety coiling up my spine. My boots squelched in the peat and the man startled, his eyes met mine and for a moment we stood in the silence like two boys, looking at each other not knowing what to do next. Suddenly he held his left leg and cried out, I rushed towards him. "It's OK" I said. I clutched the tree and slid to the ground. I gently rolled up his trousers so I could look at his leg, it was purpling already and a shard of bone jutted out viciously just above his ankle. It was bleeding heavily, and his sock and boot were saturated. I took off my sweatshirt and wrapped it around the man's leg, I tried to tie it tightly to try and stop the bleeding but he screamed and began to weep. His whole body was shaking violently and he began to gag. It was then that I heard the beginnings of muffled voices in the distance. At last. I scanned the ridgeline and I saw Nancy and Tommy leaping down the bank towards the plane wreckage.

"Over here!" I shouted to them, "We're over here!" The man shrunk even further into the tree almost as though he wished for it to swallow him whole and he started to whimper.

"No, no, please no", his accent was thick and harsh but his voice filled with child-like terror. "It's going to be fine, I promise, it will" I said and I reached out and held his hands together with mine. "We're going to get you some help, for your leg". I gestured towards his misshapen leg. The blood was beginning to seep through my sweatshirt. He looked at me with a blank and pained expression on his face, he didn't understand what I was saying but I hope he understood that I was trying to help. German or not, he was still a person, with a family, and friends, and a home, and he needed our help.

I'm sorry I didn't write yesterday, Nancy and I stayed home from school and I didn't really have the energy for writing. I kind of wanted to go really, to school, to get out of my own head and keep busy, but Edie wouldn't have it, she said we have to rest. I guess I'm still struggling to process the past few days. Nancy has barely eaten since Wednesday, she says she feels sick. She looks frightened and restless; I think she's in shock. When it happened, she ran all the way back to the village and found Mr Walters and Mr Hart in the square. They had heard the aircraft flying low across the moor but assumed it was part of the training exercise on the coast, and took little notice. When Nancy told them they all piled into Mr Hart's Land Rover and sped across the moor collecting Tommy and grandpa on the way. It took a while to cut the man free, his parachute cord was stuck in the branches and because of his leg, he was practically unable to move which made it difficult going. He had gone silent and was slowly turning a chalky white colour. I've never seen a man with so much fear in his eyes and I hope never to see it again. Mr Walters finally managed to saw through the cords and he, Tommy, Mr Hart and I set about trying to lift the man into the back of the Land Rover. He was in so much pain it broke me to hear his cries but he had lost so much blood, we had to move him otherwise he was going to bleed to death.

No one spoke on the journey to Ashburton. It was dark and I was glad not to have to look at anybody or make conversation. Nancy, Tommy and I sat in the back with the man and every time the Land Rover went over a bump he let out a feeble yelp and I could see he was holding his breath, trying to fight the pain silently. When we arrived at the Doctors house Mr Walters went ahead and knocked on the door whilst we waited outside. I couldn't hear them talking but I saw the Doctors face change and his eyes widen as he covered his mouth with both hands. He ran out to the car and opened the back of the truck,

"Come, come now, we must go to the hospital" he said. Mr Walters and Tommy lifted the man out of the Land Rover and put him straight into the Doctors car, he began to cry again and that was the last I saw of him. The Doctor shut the car door and drove away.

I've been thinking of him all day. I hope he has survived and I hope he is beginning to recover. Mr Hart said on the way back from Ashburton that I should have left him to bleed to death. I didn't know what to say so I just agreed and now I feel heavy with shame.

<u>Sunday May 2nd 1941</u>

The Doctor telephoned Edie today to thank Tommy, Nancy and I for saving the pilot's life last Wednesday. He said that he had written to the Western Morning News and he was hoping that they would write an article about what happened noting our courage and bravery. I don't feel very courageous, I just feel sad for the pilot and his family. I really hope he will make a full recovery and won't be too damaged psychologically from the accident. The Doctor said he took the pilot to the hospital in Plymouth where he is now considered a prisoner of war, but the Doctor assured Edie that he will be very well cared for until he is well again. I wish I knew his name so I could pray for him. Some of the other children at school say such awful and unkind things about the German soldiers. I know we are at war with Germany, but their soldiers are still people with feelings, personalities and emotions. They have families too, and their loss is felt just as much as our losses.

<u>Monday May 3rd 1941</u>

Everyone at school had heard about what Tommy and Nancy and I did with the German pilot last week. It was our first day back today since it happened and everybody asked us questions about it all day, it was quite a relief to get home. In morning assembly Mrs Williams asked the three of us to stand up at the front of the hall in front of everybody. She put her hand on my shoulder and said that the three of us had acted with courage, bravery and kindness and that she was very proud of each of us. She said that we saved the pilots life and without our quick thinking and valour, he would certainly have died. The whole school clapped and cheered, and whilst my cheeks turned crimson, I was brimming with pride.

Tuesday May 4th 1941

Today was just magic, totally magic. It didn't actually start that well because normally I hate my birthday so I was feeling a bit sad. This morning I waited by the farm gate for the postman to come praying that maybe I would have a letter, but I didn't. I thought maybe it was lost in the post or that maybe mum didn't know my address here. I think things do take a big longer when they're posted here because we live in the middle of the moor and our farm is so far away from any other houses. So I thought I would keep checking each morning and that hopefully something would come. I just went to school as normal and I didn't tell anyone it was my birthday and no one seemed to know so it was OK. It was just another normal day at school doing arithmetic and writing with Mrs Edwards. I even managed to read out a piece of my work to the rest of the class (even though I knew today would be a hard day) so I was very pleased with myself. I've also made a friend in my class, he's called John and he lives on a farm too but I don't think it's near ours. He hates writing too but he's really good at arithmetic so he helps me when I don't understand. Anyway, it wasn't until I got on the bus to go home with Tommy and Nancy that I began to think they were acting a bit strangely. The next strange thing that happened is that when we got off the bus at Widecombe Grandpa had come to meet us. Usually he's too busy on the farm so I wasn't expecting to see him. Grandpa, Tommy and Nancy exchanged beams and we began to walk along the lane towards the farm. The next thing that happened was just the best, really the greatest. Usually after school, I go straight to the stables to see Willow and Milly before going into the farmhouse but today Tommy led me straight into the house. When I walked in Edie was there and the whole table was covered with the most delicious birthday tea I had ever seen. Edie beamed at me and her eyes glimmered. "I've saved up my ration coupons, Harry," she said. "I've made you a special birthday tea, Grandpa will be back soon and we can all sit and celebrate, as a family". As a family, I thought. Edie said as a family. I couldn't contain my excitement any longer and I squealed and laughed, and Tommy Nancy and I all danced around the kitchen together holding hands and singing along to the radio. I hadn't felt like that for such a long time and I remember thinking, this must be happiness.

On the table there were all different sandwiches, sausage rolls and egg flan, pink jelly, sponge fingers and fruit salad. I had never seen anything like it. The kitchen was decorated with bunting and paper chains and a birthday cake with a candle in it right in the middle. Grandpa came in from milking soon after and we ate and danced and sang all evening; me, the twins, Edie and Grandpa together as a family. For the first time in a long time I felt wanted.

I'm just writing this in bed now remembering the best parts of today and feeling so lucky to be here with the Starlings at Rugglestone. I also can't really believe I'm thirteen today. I hadn't really thought about it all evening but it was my second birthday without my Dad and Jack. That's why my birthday makes me sad sometimes. I know birthdays are supposed to be fun and happy but usually for me it just marks a special time without them there, and that seems to hurt more and more with every year that passes. But today was a good birthday for the first time since the war started, and I don't think the Starling family realises quite how grateful I am for that. I hope I can repay them one day.

Thursday May 6th 1941

The best thing happened today. I had the most wonderful birthday but I was feeling a little sad because I hadn't heard anything at all from Mum. I wasn't sure if she knew my address here in Devon, and I wasn't sure if she would have sent anything anyway but I was beginning to worry. I'd heard on the radio out on the farm how bad the air raids were in London. It was all they seemed to talk about, they were calling it The Blitz and I thought that sounded quite terrible. The past couple of nights I've had a horrible dream where our house on Church Road is bombed and Mum is inside screaming to get out but she's buried by rubble and nobody can hear her. Then I wake up covered in sweat and crying and trying to get back to sleep seems impossible. This morning I waited for the dawn and went for a walk around the farm. The air was already warm and thick with the scent of gorse. Somewhere far off I could hear water toppling its way down the stream towards the village and orange sun rays pierced through the morning mist. I hauled myself up the track and when I got to the top I stopped to look around. It was just me and a little bird that danced and whirred, hopping from rock to rock and chirping as her sapphire feathers glint like oil. Everything was so still and I just stood for a moment breathing in the peace and quiet. When I got back to the farm the postman was just arriving and he handed me a bundle of post from his satchel tied together with a thread of string. I walked back across the yard flicking through the mail and that's when I saw it. There was a blue envelope addressed to me, handwritten and I was sure it was in my Mum's handwriting. I ran inside, dropped the rest of the post on the table and ripped open my envelope. It was a birthday card. I knew she wouldn't have forgotten, perhaps the post just took a little longer than she'd hoped. Inside it said:

Dearest Harry,

Happy 13th Birthday, I hope you have a wonderful day in Devon.

I am well and safe, the whole street is bombed but our little house

still stands.

Thinking of you always,

Love, Mum

I showed Edie after I'd read it and she hugged me. "Mum's never forget these things, Harry" she said and I went upstairs to get ready for school.

*

This is me writing again, Emma, this is your Grandpa. I continued to write regularly in my diary during my time in Devon, but lots of my entries were too long and uninteresting to share; and besides many sections have faded over the years leaving for difficult reading. I stayed in Devon for four years, that was four Christmases and four birthdays' with the Starling's and by the time the end of the war was nearing, I was becoming a young man myself. Although I did try to write often, I became less reliant on my diary. As a grieving young boy, it was a friend to me, and a place where I could write my darkest thoughts and worries without fear of burdening others. But the longer I spent at Rugglestone, the more I realised that I didn't need my diary anymore. I had real friends, and a family with whom I could talk to about anything in the world, I found confidence in my own voice, I didn't have to write anymore, because I could speak. I still remember those years as a very special time in my life, I remember thinking it was all too good to be true, and I have to say, very sadly it was. There's two more parts of my story Emma that I would like you to read. The first marks the beginning of the end, I remember us thinking it was all over and that our soldiers would be able to come home and everything would be right again in no time at all, but it didn't work out that way, not at all. It was over a year between the D-Day landings and the official end of the war and a long year it was.

Tommy heard it first. He came running in from the farm saying 'They've done it Mum! They've done it!' Nancy and I had just finished feeding Willow and Milly and were busily juggling breakfast and getting ready for school. Tommy's joy was infectious and before long Edie, Nancy, Tommy and I were dancing around the kitchen celebrating over orange juice and bacon sandwiches. Our boys had done it, after all their practising on the South Devon beaches not far from us, they had really gone and done it. The radio was saying it had been a success and that we had managed to occupy French beaches and would work upwards in time. We were filled to the brim with hope; this was the beginning of the end. Soon the war would be over, and although I was happy for everyone else, it embedded a feeling of dread inside of me that I had managed for so long to put to the back of my mind; I would have to go back to London. Grandpa came in about fifteen minutes later as we were tucking into our sarnies. The radio was blaring Glen Miller and Ivy

Benson and Tommy was still grinning that lovely grin. When Edie told Grandpa that the American and British army had landed in France, he went quiet and gave us all a sad sort of smile. He just put his cap back on and said 'poor fellas' before walking out onto the farm again.

I think the war has been hard for everybody in one way or another. It's different for everyone and everyone has different reasons for their heartache. I know mine, and Grandpa knows his, and I know all those boys coming back from France will have theirs, too. No one has been untouched by this war and everyone has a story to tell. Fixing the bombed out houses, streets and schools is just the beginning of it; there's a deeper level of repairing to do, and that's of the people.

<u>Wednesday 7th June 1944</u>

We had a little party at school today to celebrate the Normandy beach landings yesterday. We listened to music and played games like tag, jacks, and blind man's bluff. Tag is my favourite. The best part was we didn't do any writing or arithmetic all day and at lunch time Mrs Edwards said we could sit inside and play board games and cards and it was just so much fun. In the evening Nancy and I went for a ride on the moors and then when we got back we helped Grandpa and Tommy finish off the milking and bedding the animals down for the night. Edie made a special tea even though it isn't Friday, she said it was a day to celebrate and we had sausage meat pie with buttery mashed potato and stewed rhubarb for pudding. I came up to bed not long ago, with a full tummy and a full heart, I can't help thinking how very, very lucky I have been.

*

It's me again, Emma. I want to fast forward now just over a year to August 1945. After the success of the Normandy landings the previous summer, the radios were ringing on and on about the War nearing its end and Britain's forthcoming victory. Rather selfishly, I have to admit that this left me terrified of my impending return to Hither Green so I tried to block it out as much as I could. During my time in Devon I had been a happy child for the first time since I had lost Jack and my father. I remember looking back at the picture I had drawn at school for Mrs Parks before my evacuation and realising that Rugglestone had far exceeded my wildest dreams. I was loved and safe in a perfect world and little did I know it was all about to change for a reason that was beyond any of our remotest comprehensions. I hope these following entries aren't too difficult for you to read, Emma. I know they were difficult for me to write, but I think it's important that you see the realities of the war and the unbelievable grief it caused so many innocent people. Please don't worry yourself though Emma. I assure you, I am blessed to have had a wonderful life as the people around me have too, and what follows in my diary illustrates a darker time in what was to eventually

become a very happy life.

<u>Thursday August 16th 1945</u>

Today has been a day I prayed I would never have to live through again and I wish that I could forget it ever happened. Tommy, Grandpa and I had just finished feeding the lambs before school and we were traipsing back across the yard when it started to rain. It was one of those midsummer torrential downpours that I never knew existed until I moved to Dartmoor, and by the time we got to the farmhouse all three of us were soaked through with warm rain. We piled into the kitchen dripping wet and giggling and Edie was stood by the window, a letter grasped in one hand and the other covering her mouth as if to silence her tears. She said one word: 'James', and then I knew.

The telegram said:

```
    The Secretary of War desires me to
express his deepest
    regret that your husband Sgt. James
Robert Starling
    has been reported missing in action since
Monday 23rd July    1945.If further details or
other information are received    you will be
promptly notified.
```

Tommy turned away and walked upstairs without a word and Nancy was slumped at the kitchen table, her eyes were red and swollen. She began to cry again and Grandpa reached over and squeezed her shoulder. He kissed Edie on the cheek and walked back out onto the yard without uttering a sound. Edie said I still had to go to school, but I couldn't without the twins. I got the bus to Ashburton but when it arrived, the tears began to stream down my cheeks; the panic pressed on my chest and I couldn't breathe. I ran and ran as far away as I could until I was gasping for air. I was running from the grief but I knew it would catch me, and it did. I started to think about Dad and Jack. Jack didn't have to sign up to go to war because he was only seventeen and he worked in a steel factory in Bromley which meant that he could be exempt. But all his friends from school signed up, and so did Dad, so Jack said he felt responsibility. One day he just went and signed up and he didn't tell Mum until he got back that evening. She was angry and she said that his immature stupidity would get him killed and then she cried but I think they were angry tears. They didn't speak for quite a few days after that. I often wonder if Mum meant it. I wonder if she would take it back now after what's happened. I don't know if she would.

Jack left in October 1939 just after his seventeenth birthday and Dad left a couple of weeks after. They said they would write to me as often as they could. First of all they both went to a place near Oxford where they had two months of training. Jack's first letter came from there in late November and he sounded happy and he said the food was good and he had good friends but that it was cold at night. He said that he hadn't seen much of Dad but he saw him sometimes at mealtimes and during the evenings. He said that soon he would travel to France where he would finish his training and then begin working as a mechanic on the frontline. He was always very good working with his hands and he seemed to be able to fix everything so I knew he would be very good at this job. He sounded really excited and I wished I could have gone with him. I didn't hear from him for a while after his letters from Oxford, but I got a letter from Dad just before Christmas and he sounded cheery and optimistic, like he always was. He said France was a beautiful place and that after the war we should go there on holiday; I'd never been to another country before and it sounded so exciting. I missed them both terribly, and living at home was getting more and more unbearable. I remember the day Jack's telegram came because the postman was late so I went to school before I found out. It was a Friday in late March 1940 and we were halfway through English when Mr Harris came into the class and asked to speak to me. He looked stern so I thought maybe I was in big trouble because the day before I had hid during gym and Mrs Parks couldn't find me. So I was preparing myself for a scolding when he just blurted it out. I didn't really hear it at first; or maybe I just didn't believe it. The pain scoured me hollow, but I didn't cry, I couldn't cry, this was beyond tears. I don't remember much of what happened after that. I didn't go to school for a while and mum didn't go to work. Mum's friends brought flowers to the house in their hundreds. They flooded our little house like an ocean; wildflowers, poppies and daisies, daffodils and sharp yellow tulips. The poppies wilted first, then the tulips. The daffodils were last to go crisp and curl at the edges before dropping to the floor and joining the wave of charred petals throughout the house that would not be swept up for months. Mrs Parks brought a pie because she said we still had to eat. I think she must have saved up her ration coupons because it had a buttery thick pastry crust and was filled to the brim. She looked pale and tired and she said she hoped I would feel able to come back to school soon. But we couldn't eat it; it sat on the counter for days and days untouched wilting and drying with each hour. Mum spent her days smoking leant up against the stove, cigarette after cigarette and the whole kitchen was overflowing with old smoke and sadness. She didn't even register me anymore. I wasn't a person to her; I just became a reminder, a younger version of Jack, my face bringing it all back to her again and again and the guilt ate me from the inside out. It had been three weeks since Jack's telegram had come, and I was just beginning to think about going back to school. Mum was beginning to spend more and more time in bed and I felt so helpless. I wanted to look after her but I desperately needed to get out of the house. I remember the morning it happened because it was a beautiful, warm spring day so I decided to try get out and go for a walk in the park. The trees were beginning to burst into a canopy of green and children played happily on the green. For the first time since Jack had died, I'd manage to forget about it, just for a few moments, and in those few moments, I felt like a normal boy again. I was walking back along our street and I saw a shiny, black car parked outside our house and a man in uniform stood at the door. He was knocking but Mum hadn't answered. At first I thought perhaps there had been news of Jack, maybe they had made a mistake? Maybe he was alive, perhaps he had just been injured and not killed? Hundreds of thoughts tore through my mind as I rushed up the garden path to the door, I had a tiny glimmer of hope and I was hanging on to it and praying with everything I had. I pushed the door and shouted for mum, but she didn't come. I turned back to the man at the door and he passed me a telegram.

"Sincerest condolences young man" he said and he took one step back before turning and walking away.

That was the moment everything unravelled and I fell deeper than I thought possible. I will never forget reading the telegram and having to go upstairs and give it to Mum. She was lying half under the covers smoking and still in her nightgown. The bedroom reeked of stale smoke and old perfume.

"It's Dad" I said, "He's missing". My voice cracked and before I had a chance to say anything else she howled in pain and curled up on the bed like a child, the ash from her cigarette burning the bed sheets. I lay on the bed next to her and I don't remember anything after that for weeks.

<u>Wednesday August 22nd 1945</u>

They say on the radio that the end of the war is nearing but it's not for us. There's still no news of James and Edie is beginning to lose hope. I can see the helplessness in her eyes and her bravery is fading fast. We haven't spoken about it Nancy and I. We haven't spoken much at all. Everything at Rugglestone has been turned upside down by James' disappearance and each day without news is another day of heartache. I think Edie fears the worst and needs closure, and I'm pretty sure Grandpa does too, but Tommy won't speak. I just want to make it better but I can't. Nothing I can do will ever fill the void, I know that from experience.

Sunday September 2nd 1945

Today should be a happy day, a day where we can celebrate. The war has ended, and we should be joyful, and looking forward towards a better future. But instead we all feel empty. My brother isn't coming home, and neither is my Dad and that sad truth is a reality for so many people all over the country. There's a huge void left in so many of our lives and it's never going to be filled ever again. Grandpa turned the radio off in the barns today. It hurt him too much I don't think he could bear to hear it anymore. We all walked to Widecombe this evening and the whole village sat together in the church whilst the bells rang for the first time since the start of the war. The sound bounced off the hills surrounding the village and echoed in harmony all around us and we all bowed our heads in silence. We prayed for the lost men, the injured and the missing and we vowed together that it would not be in vain. We prayed for the Harper family who run the inn and lost their youngest son, Rowan. He was only eighteen. We prayed for Mr and Mrs

Parker from the village shop who lost both of their sons during the Normandy landings, and Mrs Walters who lost her husband; they had only been married two years. Then we all prayed for James; Mr. James Starling of Rugglestone Farm who is missing in action presumed deceased and Edie crumpled into Tommy and silently wept, and there was nothing any of us could do to possibly make it better.

<u>Tuesday September 11th 1945</u>

I've barely slept since the telegram came. The nights are long and
hot, and even the early morning air is thick and heavy. It's been
three weeks and still we've heard nothing. Grandpa bought my train
ticket back to Paddington today when he went to town but he said he
would look after it for me until the weekend. Tommy spends most of
his time out on the farm now and I barely see him. I want more than
anything to talk to him, but I don't know what I can possibly say to
make it better. Grandpa puts on a brave face most days but I can see
the veneer is beginning to crack and it breaks my heart. I'm trying to
help out around the house and out on the farm but I just feel that I
get in the way and I wonder if maybe it might be better for them
when I go back to London. I often sit in the barn with Willow and
Milly and think. I always drift into my own little fantasy world,
thinking about Mum and Dad and Jack. I squint and look out across
the yard and towards the village. The long grass in the fields ebbs
and flows like waves and I think about everything I've ever lost

since the beginning of the war. If I wait long enough, maybe Dad and Jack will walk onto the yard and help Grandpa and Tommy with the evening milk, or maybe Mum will come and help Edie feed the lambs. Mum would be smiling and laughing like she used to, and in the evening we'd eat around the table and she'd hug me and squeeze me tight telling me how proud of me she is. The dream never went any further than that, I never let it. I had to haul myself back to reality and just wait for a moment in the barn stroking Willow and composing myself before heading back into the house to help Edie with dinner.

<u>Thursday September 13th 1945</u>

Two nights left before I have to go back. Nancy and I spent the evening sat in the meadow on the edge of the farm looking over towards Haytor and Hound Tor rocks. It's my favourite place on the farm because on a clear day Dartmoor stretches out infinitely in front of you and it makes me feel like I am on top of the world. Tonight the sky streaked scarlet across a cold and pale backdrop and the moorland was tinted amber as the sun set beneath the hills. There were sheep grazing in the meadow where we sat and the way they teared at the grass so rhythmically filled the sad silence that suffocated us. I kept glancing at Nancy to check she was OK and when she looked back at me I saw the fear and despair in her eyes. "He'll come home won't he Harry?" Her eyes bulging with tears and she wiped them away with her sleeve. I had no words. My father never came home, and neither did my brother so what hope could I possibly give to Nancy? I leant over and kissed her cheek, took her hand and lead her back home. There was nothing I could say or do to give her the reassurance she needed and that broke my heart.

<u>Saturday September 15th 1945</u>

I wish I could forget today. I wish it never happened and that I was still at Rugglestone with Tommy, Nancy, Edie and Grandpa, feeding the calves and shearing sheep. My train left at 9 o'clock so I should be back at Hither Green by 4 o'clock. I don't know what I'll say to Mum; I guess she will be at work anyway. I keep trying to block out Tommy's face when they left the station this morning but I can't. Tommy is always so cheery and happy but since the telegram came he's been so quiet. None of us spoke on the bus journey to Ashburton. Haytor and Hound Tor were amber in the early sunlight and the ground was all glittery with dewdrops. There were ponies grazing with wet backs and sheep lying huddled together under gorse and bracken and I remembered when we camped out on the moor with Grandpa during lambing. I remembered all our journeys to school on this bus, and I tried to imagine that it was just another school day and not the last time I would ever see Dartmoor and Rugglestone and be with Tommy, Nancy, Edie and Grandpa. I was trying so hard to swallow back the tears the whole way and when the bus pulled up in Ashburton, I turned and saw Nancy had already been crying. I reached out and squeezed her hand but she didn't squeeze back. When we got to the station it was really quiet and Tommy carried my suitcase for me. We stood on the platform looking at each other. We had been so inseparable for nearly four whole years and it was about to end yet none of us could think of a word to say. I looked around and I just remember feeling like I belonged there on Dartmoor with them. London had become a dangerous and daunting place in my mind, where I had been a frightened and timid little boy, so afraid of the world and so alone. Here it was so different. I'd become a young man, I felt confident, I felt valued and wanted but most of all I felt loved. A few minutes passed before the station master blew his whistle and I knew it was time. I turned to hug Nancy. Tommy joined in too and we stood for a moment just holding each other with no words adequate to say what we felt. The tears spilled down my cheeks but I didn't wipe them away. After a moment I let go of Nancy and took my suitcase from Tommy's hand.

"Go", I said, "it's OK". It wasn't though. The pain left me without breath, like a kick in the chest, and I felt numb and empty. Tommy turned back but Nancy held his arm, his eyes were full of tears. "I want you to stay Harry, please know I wish you could stay", and then without another sound, they turned and walked away. The trees were just beginning to turn for autumn and in the breeze their browning underbellies flashed upwards towards the sky. I saw the train coming in the distance and I just stood there for a while staring. I began to imagine a world where everything I had ever wanted wasn't torn from in front of me. I half closed my eyes and I thought I would wake up in the barn where Nancy, Tommy and I had slept during lambing. We'd be wrapped up in old blankets covered in straw and Edie would bring us tea and sausages for breakfast and the dogs would come and sit with us and everything would be OK. We'd milk the cows and feed the lambs and then walk to the village to get the bus to school. When we got home we'd ride the ponies out and gallop through the bracken and over the moors, it would be me and the twins against the whole world and nothing would ever tear us apart. Even though I knew that it was just a dream, and the tears rolled down my face, it was a thought that kept me safe. I thought that whenever I felt scared or unsure, I would close my eyes and imagine how I had wanted the story to end. The train hissed

alongside the platform and without looking back I stepped on. I

couldn't even think about Rugglestone anymore, I was heading back

to Mum's little house on Church Road and I had to try and forget.

So that's where my diary ended, Emma. I packed it away when I got back to Hither Green and I never wanted to open it again. I thought it would open too many wounds and the thought of Devon and Tommy and Nancy broke my heart again and again. I never found out whether James came home and I was too scared to write in case a reply brought the news I desperately longed not to hear. So I didn't. I tried so hard to forget, and although it tore me apart, I saw it as the only way. I remember Mum was at work when I got back to Church Road and the house was locked so I used the key from behind the gate and let myself in. It was like I had never been away; everything was the same, even Mum's cigarettes and lipstick on the side by the stove. In my room, the bed sheets were made neatly and my school uniform was folded on the chair at the bottom of the bed. It didn't seem like four years had passed since I had worn it last. I don't really remember what happened over the few weeks following my return to Hither Green, I just remember Mum was thinner and paler, and smoked much more than I had remembered. She never asked me about Devon so I never told her. I often wondered over the years what she thought about my evacuation. I used to think perhaps it was a relief for her, I always felt she would have preferred me to have been out of the way, to give her space after losing her eldest son and husband in such quick succession. It wasn't until I watched over her on her death bed many years later that I finally understood that her anger towards me as a child was the only outlet for her unimaginable pain and suffering. I forgave her then, and she died peacefully later that night at the grand old age of 90; that was two years before you were born, Emma, and I know she would have loved to have met you. After the war ended, London gradually went back to normal, I remember tearing down the blackout blinds and heaving sandbags into the street to be collected. For a while, it was a sad place to be. The shells of homes, even whole streets in places, were an eerie reminder of what the country had been through, and people were shadows of their former selves, pale and frightened; no one really smiled or laughed anymore. I remember when Hither Green School opened again in December 1945 after the hall was rebuilt. Mum said it had been bombed to shreds just weeks after the last class of children had been evacuated. Mrs Parks came back to teach us and her warmth and support filled the huge hole in our lives and repaired the trauma of the previous few years of war. She

continued to teach me until I was sixteen and I tried to keep in touch

with her after I left. She retired soon after and stayed in Hither

Green with her husband for the rest of her life. She died in 1986 and

whenever I visit London now I always make sure to put flowers on

her gravestone. I left school in 1948 with a few qualifications but I

really didn't know which path I wanted to take in life. I enjoyed

writing and drawing but I wasn't intelligent enough to work in the

city and besides, I had no desire to work indoors, so I took up a job

with Westminster council. That meant getting the underground into

central London each morning, and working tirelessly in the parks;

gardening, tidying, cleaning pathways and sweeping leaves. It was

hard work, but I needed that. My twenty-fifth birthday came and

passed and I was still living on Church Road with Mum working

every hour God gave. I never did forget about Rugglestone Farm

and the Starling's, and one evening when I was catching the bus

back to Hither Green dreaming about Dartmoor, I had an idea. I

would save up my wages and my leave, and I would catch a train

west to Ashburton and visit all the places I knew when I lived there

nearly thirteen years before. I hadn't spoken to Nancy or Tommy since I left and I didn't want to interfere with their adult lives or

bring up old wounds with the disappearance of James, (and besides,

they might not have even remembered me). So, I decided I would just

go quietly and spend time on my own exploring Devon from a new

and different perspective. That was in June 1957 and in the October

of that year I finally plucked up the courage to buy my train ticket

west. I packed my things in Dad's old suitcase just like before, and

caught the bus to Paddington, making sure to stop off at the

cemetery to tell Dad and Jack about my upcoming adventure and

tidy their graves from the falling autumn leaves. I remember the

journey so vividly, the greyed sharp edges of London slowly fading

to soft greens, ambers, and golds, clear rivers and curved hillsides.

The evening was drawing in and as the train rushed alongside the

crimson cliffs of the East Devon coastline, the sun melted into the

horizon and I remember feeling so at home. It must have been gone

dark by the time the train pulled in at Newton Abbot, as I remember

deciding to find an inn and spend the night there before heading

towards Ashburton and Dartmoor the following day. Now you know

Ashburton well, Emma, from all your summer holidays spent here

with me and your grandma at Rugglestone Cottage, so I hope you can imagine the next part of my story when I try to explain it to you in words the best I can. I hope it will be a surprise to you, as it still was to me for many, many years. I travelled to Ashburton on the bus the following morning from Newton Abbot and I remember it being a particularly blustery cold autumn day. When I arrived it must have been about 9 o'clock; I stopped for breakfast at the old White Hart Inn on the main street and it started to rain. I spent the best part of the morning wandering around the town in the drizzle. It hadn't really changed in the time I had been gone, and it was just like I was twelve again walking to school with Tommy and Nancy. I remember feeling rather wet and cold and thinking I ought to be getting back to Newton Abbot; and that's when I saw her. She hadn't changed one bit, she just looked older, gentler, and more mature. Her hair was still the same mousy brown and loosely curled, and the small pink birthmark on her cheek, more faded now, but still there. It was Nancy. Nancy Starling, who I said goodbye to almost thirteen years ago exactly and thought I would never see again. She was walking towards me shopping bags in hand, wearing muddy wellingtons, with a collie dog by her side. I stopped in the street frozen to the spot and when she looked at me I saw her face change from curiosity to

shock to disbelief, and I knew then that she knew it was me. She
stopped and put down her bags.

"Harry?" she said. I was looking down at my worn shoes and I
could feel my face burning crimson. I couldn't find the words to say.
"Harry Clarke from London, is that you?" I looked up and smiled
that same goofy smile that hadn't changed since I was twelve and
Nancy covered her mouth with her hands and her eyes filled with
tears. I swallowed back my own and cleared my throat.

"Nancy?" I whispered hesitantly, and the tears rolled down my
cheeks. I don't really remember much of what happened after that. It
was all a blur of tears and hugs and laughter and memories. Nancy
took me back to Rugglestone Farm that afternoon and I remember
my head nearly reaching the rafters and having to duck as I walked
through the doorways. Tommy did too. He was a grown man, tall
and broad and strong, but his face was the same and his eyes still lit
up in that same way that they did all those years ago; and then there
was James. He looked like Tommy, and had the same kind blue eyes,
but he was older, greyer, with aged skin and much less hair. I found
out later that he had been a prisoner of war, injured and
hospitalised under German care and he was released on September

2nd, 1945 before returning home to Widecombe and Rugglestone

only weeks after I had left. I remember him saying that Tommy had

written about me in his letters to France, and that he felt I had been

a part of the family all along. Grandpa Starling passed away

peacefully at the farm in 1955; Edie said he never stopped working

until the day he died and he always remembered little blonde Harry

Clarke from London who had never seen a lamb. He was buried in

Widecombe churchyard under the big oak tree and that evening

Nancy, Tommy and I walked to the village to see his grave and talk

properly, just the three of us. It was just like before, like we had

never been apart, and how my heart glowed, Emma. I really hadn't

felt happiness like it since I was a boy on the farm. At last, I felt

whole again. I don't know if you can guess what happens next

Emma, but I never did go back to Hither Green. Not to stay anyway,

only a week or so later to collect my things and Nancy came with me

to meet mum, too. We visited Dad and Jack and Mrs Parks on the

way back to Paddington, and Nancy stood with me and helped me

clear their graves. I didn't want to say goodbye, but I knew that they

would have been so proud of me. I wasn't sure when I would be

back, but I realised then that it didn't really matter, because they were there with me wherever I went and I would always hold them close. I moved to Devon in November 1957 and I started working on the farm with Tommy and James that winter. Nancy was nearing the end of teacher training, and she qualified in the New Year. She got a job teaching at the new primary school in Buckland-in-the-Moor and together, we bought a cottage on the moor between Widecombe and Buckland. It needed a lot of work doing to it, so between us and Tommy, we spent much of 1958 tirelessly working the farm and trying to do up the cottage at the same time. It was a busy time, and tiring too, but it was wonderful to be with them Emma, it really was. Dartmoor meant the world to me, and still does now, but really what made it home were Edie and James, Tommy and Nancy. It was them who I had been missing all along and at last, once more I felt whole. Nancy and I married in spring 1959 in the church at Widecombe where you were christened, Emma, and it was a perfect day. Everyone came; even your great-grandmother came down from Hither Green and stayed for the week; and she too was filled to the brim with gentle kindness by the Starlings. On that warm April afternoon Nancy Starling became Nancy Clarke and we never looked back.

I don't know if you remember the farm Emma. You spent a lot of time there with me, your Grandma and your Mum and Dad when you were much younger, but after many happy years living at Rugglestone and working the land, we decided it was time to sell up in 2005 as it was becoming just too much for Tommy and I to manage. So that's when we moved down to the cottage in Ashburton. We named it Rugglestone Cottage as a tribute to our wonderful, wonderful farm and we made a vow to each other that we would never forget. I often still visit the farm now and sit beneath the three silver birch trees that I planted in memory of my brother Jack, your great-grandfather, Albert, and my affectionate brother-in-law and best friend, Tommy. They stand on the edge of the farm looking east towards Haytor, and the moorland stretches out indefinitely beneath them, glowing in the amber sunlight. In the evening, dusk pulls at the daylight and long shadows of tors are cast out across Dartmoor. Ponies rest and sheep cluster together beneath bracken and gorse. From there I write this very letter for you, Emma, and I know that you'll be able to imagine it when you read this. Maybe I'll bring you here yourself one day soon, and we'll plant a silver birch tree for your grandmother and my sweetheart Nancy Starling, and there she will rest and look out over Dartmoor forever and ever.

With love always,

Your affectionate grandfather,

Harry

The end

With thanks to all those who helped me to write this book, in particular, Stephen Moss, Miriam Darlington, Min Wild, Deborah Burrell, Zoe Walters, Rosie Sice, my family, my brother Jamie for the beautiful cover photograph, and most of all, Peg and everyone at Erme Valley Riding for the Disabled who have always believed in me.

Printed in Great Britain
by Amazon

79486965R00073